Epilepsy

Epilepsy

Elaine Landau

TWENTY-FIRST CENTURY BOOKS

A Division of Henry Holt and Company
New York

Twenty-First Century Books
A Division of Henry Holt and Company, Inc.
115 West 18th Street
New York, NY 10011

Henry Holt ® and colophon are trademarks of
Henry Holt and Company, Inc.
Publishers since 1866

Published in Canada by Fitzhenry & Whiteside Ltd.,
195 Allstate Parkway, Markham, Ontario, L3R 4T8

Library of Congress Cataloging-in-Publication Data
Landau, Elaine.
Epilepsy / Elaine Landau. — 1st ed.
p. cm. — (Understanding illness)
Includes index.
1. Epilepsy—Juvenile literature. [1. Epilepsy. 2. Diseases.]
I. Title. II Series: Landau, Elaine. Understanding illness.
RC372.L295 1994
616.8'53—dc20 94-13833
CIP
AC

ISBN 0-8050-2991-5
First Edition 1994

Printed in the United States of America
All first editions are printed on acid-free paper ∞.
10 9 8 7 6 5 4 3 2 1

Photo Credits
pp. 12 (both), 19, 22: Dan McCoy/Rainbow; pp. 14, 20, 33: Ilo E. Leppik, M.D.; p. 16: National Library of Medicine; pp. 26, 41: Tom McCarthy/Transparencies, Inc.; p. 35: Terry Wild Studio; p. 36: Randy Kalisek/Light Writings; p. 43: Camerique/H. Armstrong Roberts; p. 51: Carl Purcell.

For Michael Brent Pearl

CONTENTS

Epilepsy

CHAPTER ONE

Epilepsy

It happened in the cafeteria of the junior high Jeff Sanders (name changed) attended. The 11-year-old boy uttered a single cry as he fell to the floor. He immediately lost consciousness, but his body thrashed about in violent spasms. Unable to swallow the saliva that collected in his throat and mouth, it flowed from the young boy's lips in what looked like a foam.

The attack that gripped Jeff was over minutes later. He regained consciousness, exhausted by what he'd been through and embarrassed that it had happened in school in front of his classmates and friends. Although he was momentarily dazed afterward, Jeff knew what had occurred. It had happened to him before. Jeff Sanders has epilepsy and he had just experienced a seizure.

Epilepsy is a medical term used to describe more than 20 different kinds of conditions characterized by seizures. The seizures are brought on by small groups of damaged overactive neurons (nerve cells) in the brain. Under normal circumstances brain cells send messages to one another through electrical signals, or impulses. The cells "fire" in an orderly and controlled manner. But during a seizure damaged cells fire strong, rapid electrical charges that disrupt the brain's normal functioning.

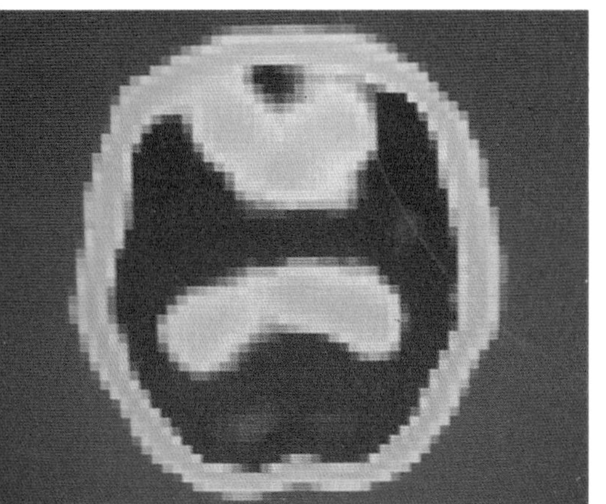
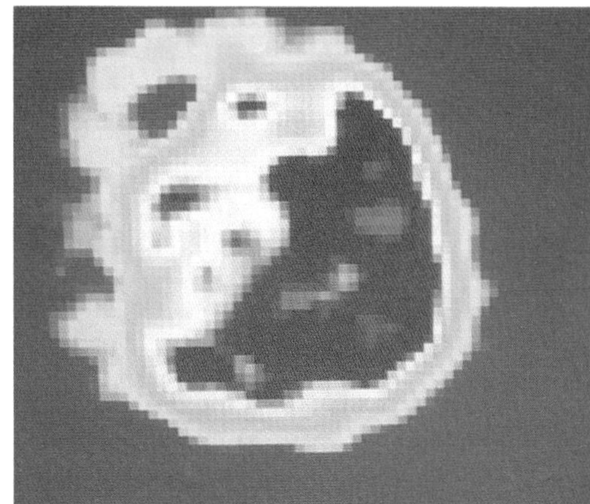

A PET scan of a normally functioning brain (left).
A PET scan of an epileptic seizure (right).

Epileptic seizures have sometimes been compared to a lightning storm in the person's brain or a platoon of soldiers all firing their weapons at once. Normal nerve cells fire electrical impulses at a rate of up to 80 times a second. But during a seizure epileptic neurons discharge up to 500 times a second.

There are many different types of seizures. The kind of seizure a person has generally depends on where in the brain neurons fire uncontrollably and how far the rapid firing has spread. If the abnormal activity occurs only in one part of the brain, the seizure is usually described as partial.

There are various kinds of partial seizures. At times seizures known as "complex partial" affect the emotional centers of the brain, causing the person to cry or feel angry or afraid for no apparent reason. If the portion of the brain responsible for sound or sight is involved, the person may experience auditory or visual hallucinations (hear or see things that aren't real).

Unfortunately in some instances people having complex partial seizures are thought to be drunk, on drugs, or mentally ill. That's because the seizure may cause them to appear to act irrationally. They may seem dazed, chew even though they're not eating, talk to themselves, pull at their clothing, or not respond to those around them. As one 15-year-old California boy described what it was like to undergo these seizures, "It was humiliating. I was drug-tested two times because school officials assumed my seizures were the result of alcohol or drugs."[1] Naturally the test results were negative each time. However, in these situations it may still be difficult to shake off the unsettling suspicions of teachers and classmates.

Dr. Margery S. Ashley, director of Epilepsy Services of Northeastern Illinois, noted that complex partial seizures are often seen in teenagers. She further described the possible social consequences of these attacks as follows: "Complex partial seizures frequently [make the person] appear bizarre. And sometimes the response [of others to the person] can be very inappropriate. For instance, someone might call the police after witnessing another person have a complex partial seizure."[2]

Another broad category of epileptic seizures is generalized seizures. Unlike partial seizures, in generalized seizures the whole brain is flooded with intense electrical signals. There are also different kinds of generalized seizures. But perhaps the one most often associated with

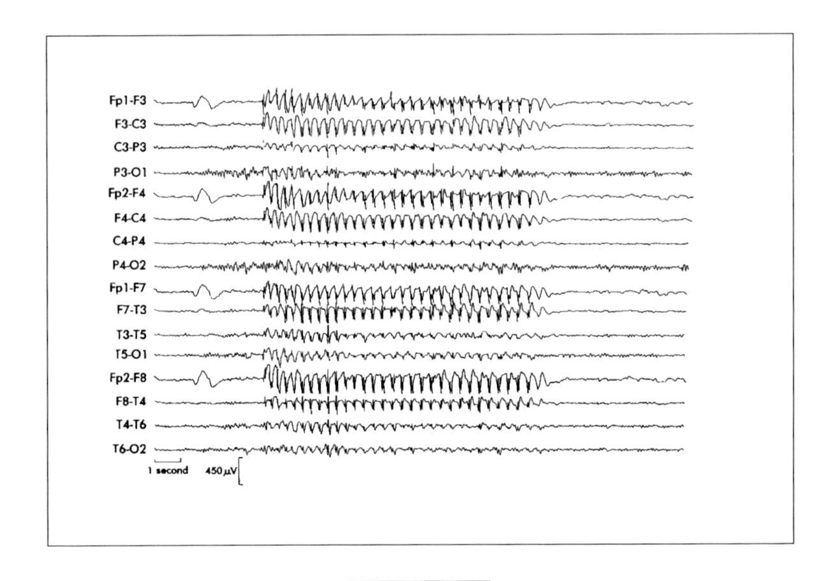

The center of this electroencephalogram (EEG) shows brain waves during an absence seizure (formerly known as petit mal). Normal brain waves were recorded on either side.

epilepsy is the tonic-clonic seizure (formerly known as grand mal) that Jeff Sanders experienced in his junior-high school's cafeteria. The absence seizure (formerly known as petit mal) is another kind of generalized seizure but it's considerably less dramatic. During these attacks the person may merely seem momentarily distracted. It might look as if he or she has been daydreaming, or in some cases, the seizure may even go unnoticed.

Yet these seizures can still be troublesome for those who have them. Lisa, an intelligent 15-year-old high-school student, had suffered from absence seizures for some time. In her case there were no obvious symptoms, she just seemed to be briefly "out of it." Then following the seizure, Lisa would go back to what she was doing. However, before Lisa's epilepsy was identified and treated, the seizures came so often that she was unable to concentrate in school. Trying to cope with these attacks several hundred times a day, Lisa fell far behind in her work and was in danger of having to repeat her grade. She felt so frightened and ashamed of what was happening to her that she even refused to tell any of her friends what was wrong.[3]

Epilepsy is not a new disorder. In fact there have been descriptions of it since the beginning of recorded history. The ancient Greeks believed epileptic seizures were actually visitations from the gods. It was called "the sacred disease" and those who had it were thought to be blessed. People with epilepsy were less highly regarded during the Renaissance. At that time evil demons were believed to be behind the seizures and the person experiencing them was thought to be possessed by the devil. Unfortunately, many people with epilepsy were burned at the stake after being accused of being sorcerers.

Even just a century ago things were still extremely difficult for individuals with epilepsy. There were few available treatments and these patients were frequently shunned, as it was mistakenly thought that their ailment was contagious. Often people with epilepsy were shut away in hospitals or sanatoriums confined to "epileptics only."

It wasn't until some mid-nineteenth century pioneering neurologists (doctors who treat disorders and diseases of the brain and spinal cord) turned their attention to epilepsy that real progress in treatment began.

Dr. John Hughlings Jackson, 1835-1911

Among them was a British physician named John Hughlings Jackson. In 1870 Dr. Jackson noted that the cerebral cortex, or outer layer of the brain, was a factor in the disorder. He further realized that rapidly firing nerve cells produced seizures.

Since that time many significant advances have been achieved. This book is about what's been accomplished and the challenges that lie ahead both in conquering this disorder and the stigma often attached to it.

CHAPTER TWO

Diagnosing and Treating Epilepsy

An ill four-year-old boy with a high fever has a seizure for the first time in his life. Does this mean that he has epilepsy?

Not necessarily. At times children running high fevers may experience convulsions. Similarly, adults have had seizures in reaction to various drugs prescribed for them as well as for other reasons. However, these individuals cannot be thought to have epilepsy unless they experience further seizures when these special conditions are not present.

In the past the diagnosis of epilepsy was often less than perfect. It's estimated that as many as a fifth of those thought to have it did not. On the other hand, some young people experiencing absence seizures were frequently misdiagnosed as having a learning disability or even thought to be mentally retarded.

The situation has improved in recent years. Today in diagnosing epilepsy the physician will be guided by both the patient's history and the results of the medical tests administered. It's also relevant that 75 percent of those with epilepsy had their first seizure before turning 18 years of age. Therefore when a parent brings in a child who's had a seizure, the parent will be asked to describe the symptoms as well as the seizure's length. The parent must also supply the doctor with full background information on the young person's present health and medical history.

While such information can be extremely helpful, most doctors will also want the patient to take a test known as an EEG (electroencephalogram). An EEG shows whether or not there is abnormal brain activity that may result in seizures. To take the test, thin wires (electrodes) from a machine called an electroencephalograph are attached to the patient's scalp. The electroencephalograph indicates the type of electrical activity occurring in the person's brain through a series of wavy lines recorded on a moving sheet of paper. If the electrical activity is normal, a recognizable pattern will appear. But irregular patterns may indicate seizure-causing changes. An EEG is a painless procedure that is done in a doctor's office and usually takes between 35 and 40 minutes.

Although the EEG may be the test most often used to diagnose epilepsy, it isn't always completely reliable. That's because with some forms of the condition it may record normal brain waves if taken when the person isn't having a seizure. Therefore physicians may also have their patients take other tests before arriving at a diagnosis.

Among these is the CAT scan, which stands for computerized axial tomography. A CAT scan is actually a computerized three-dimensional X-ray image of the brain. It can be particularly helpful in ruling out other conditions such as a brain tumor, a cyst, or excess fluid

A young patient undergoing an electroencephalogram (EEG).

in the brain, which can also cause seizures. At times such underlying conditions can be treated and the seizures will stop.

In recent years new types of scans have been developed. These often provide physicians with more information about what's happening in the brain. One such test is called an MRI, or magnetic resonance imaging. In

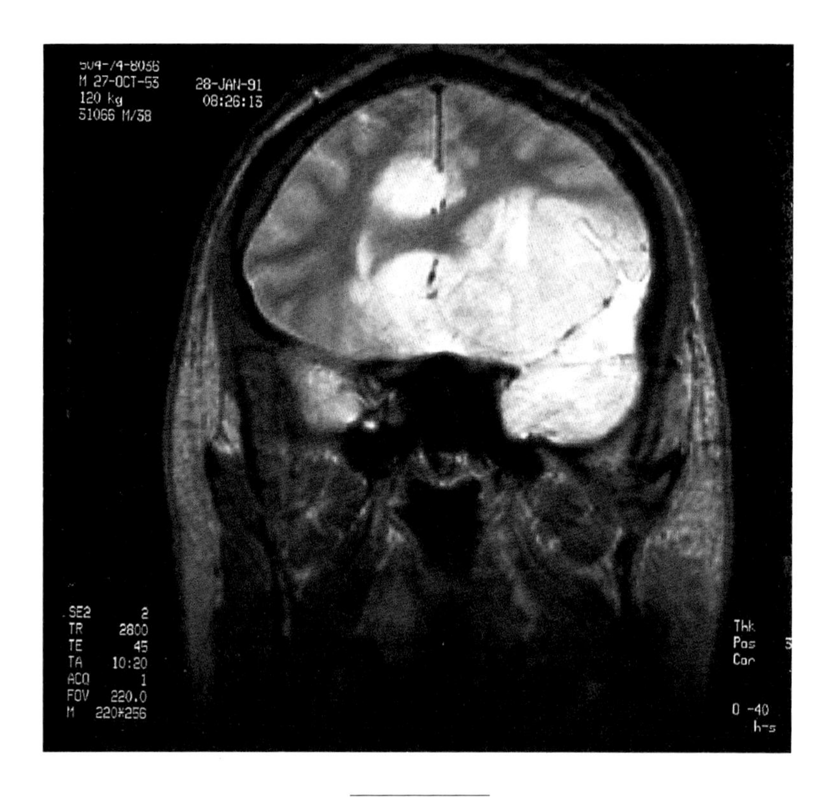

This MRI of a patient's brain allows doctors to more readily pinpoint problems.

this procedure magnetic fields rather than X rays offer sharp, revealing pictures of the brain. Still another test that's now being used is the PET scan, or positron-emission tomography. The PET scan differs from other tests in that it provides color-coded pictures of the brain at work.

Once a diagnosis has been reached, the physician must devise a treatment plan for the patient. At times people with epilepsy may be put on a ketogenic diet in which they eat foods with a high fat content. The diet creates a condition in the body known as ketosis, which some believe inhibits seizures. A ketogenic diet is supposed to be especially helpful to children with epilepsy. However, this method of treatment is not widely used because the diet is expensive and most patients dislike the foods. While high-fat foods such as whipped cream may sound delicious, they are not very tasty when made without sugar, as on this diet. Having to prepare separate meals can be difficult for the patient's family as well.

A psychological approach has also been tried in treating epilepsy. This involves training people with epilepsy to control their brain waves through a technique known as biofeedback. Biofeedback involves monitoring certain biological factors such as brain waves, blood pressure, heart rate, and skin temperature through the use of electronic instruments. This information is conveyed, or "fed back," to the patient, who has been taught specific techniques to alter these bodily functions to a lower, relaxed level. Patients with epilepsy attempt to change their brain's electrical activity by modifying certain images and sounds in their minds. Although biofeedback has been beneficial to some patients, scientists still don't precisely understand why it works.

The majority of patients with epilepsy control their seizures through prescription drugs. Some antiepileptic drugs suppress or stop the damaged nerve cells' undesirable activity. Others act to lessen the responsiveness of the surrounding normal cells in order to limit the spread of the excessive electrical discharge to other areas of the brain. The use of drugs first began in 1857 when Sir

Some people with epilepsy have successfully used biofeedback (as shown here) to control their brain waves and reduce the number of seizures they experience.

Charles Locock, an English physician, introduced bromides for use in such cases. Locock found that bromides had a soothing effect on his patients and considerably reduced their seizures.

More than half a century later in 1912, physicians began prescribing another sedative (a drug that produces a calming effect) called phenobarbital for their patients with epilepsy. Phenobarbital and other similar drugs were an improvement over the bromides. They proved to be superior at controlling the seizures, and the patients experienced fewer negative side effects. However, these early drugs weren't the answer for everyone. Although they were effective at controlling various types of partial seizures and tonic-clonic seizures, they had little or no effect on absence seizures.

Today the situation has vastly improved. There are presently more than 20 different anticonvulsant, or antiepileptic, medications approved for use in the United States. In most cases these drugs largely prevent epileptic seizures from occurring. In August 1993 a new drug known as felbamate was made available to patients experiencing partial seizures. National Institute of Neurological Disorders and Strokes (NINDS) director Murray Goldstein described felbamate as "the first major antiepileptic agent to be introduced into the United States since 1977."[1] The drug is expected to benefit about half of all Americans who suffer from epilepsy. Felbamate differs from other antiepileptic drugs currently used in that it is safe even at high doses. In addition to this medication, four other anticonvulsant drugs should be available within the next few years. However, no drug can cure epilepsy. When taken regularly antiepileptic drugs merely bring the seizures under control.

The type of medicine prescribed depends on the kind of seizures the patient has. In some cases two or more drugs may be needed to achieve the goal. Someone who experiences more than one kind of seizure may have to take more than one drug as well. Yet whenever possible the doctor will try to control the condition with the smallest dosage of the least number of drugs.

At times it may be difficult to immediately identify the best medication for a patient. That's because people react to drugs in varied ways. A drug that effectively controls seizures for one patient may do little for another. The time it takes a drug to become fully effective also differs among people. Some patients find that their medication works almost immediately, while for others more time is needed. Often a doctor may have to raise or lower a patient's drug dose or try several drugs before finding the right one.

Individuals also experience different side effects to the medications prescribed. Common side effects of antiepileptic drugs include fatigue, irritability, nausea, rashes, and poor coordination. A few medications may produce mood changes and learning or behavioral difficulties. At times a drug that is wrong for a patient can bring on seizures instead of stopping them.

Some patients find the side effects they experience bearable. One young girl whose medication made her tired found taking a short nap before dinner to be helpful. Others must be switched to another medication. There is also a substantial number of people who take these drugs for extended periods and never experience any ill effects.

It's important to be monitored by a doctor while taking antiepileptic medication. Monitoring involves having a blood sample taken to determine the level of the drug present in the patient's bloodstream. This helps the physician determine the best drug dosage to control the patient's seizures. Blood samples are usually taken in the beginning of the treatment as well as once the correct level of the drug for the patient has been identified. If there's a significant change in the patient's well-being, drug-level tests may be repeated.

People on antiepileptic drugs must be sure their doctor knows about any other medication they may be taking. At times drugs used for an entirely different medical problem can heighten or weaken the anticonvulsant's effect. This is especially important for women taking antiepileptic medication as well as birth control pills. If the two drugs are used together, sometimes both become less potent. When taking over-the-counter drugs, it's also important for people on antiepileptic medications to ask their pharmacist or physician how this will effect their prescription medication.

In some instances other factors can make people decide whether or not to take anticonvulsants. This may be especially so for pregnant women since there's evidence that some antiepileptic drugs can increase the risks of birth defects in the unborn child. Pregnant women who experience seizures often find themselves in a difficult position, since their attacks are likely to continue if they stop their medication. Unfortunately, a seizure can endanger the fetus in other ways. If the woman has difficulty breathing during an attack, the baby might be deprived of oxygen, which could result in brain damage.

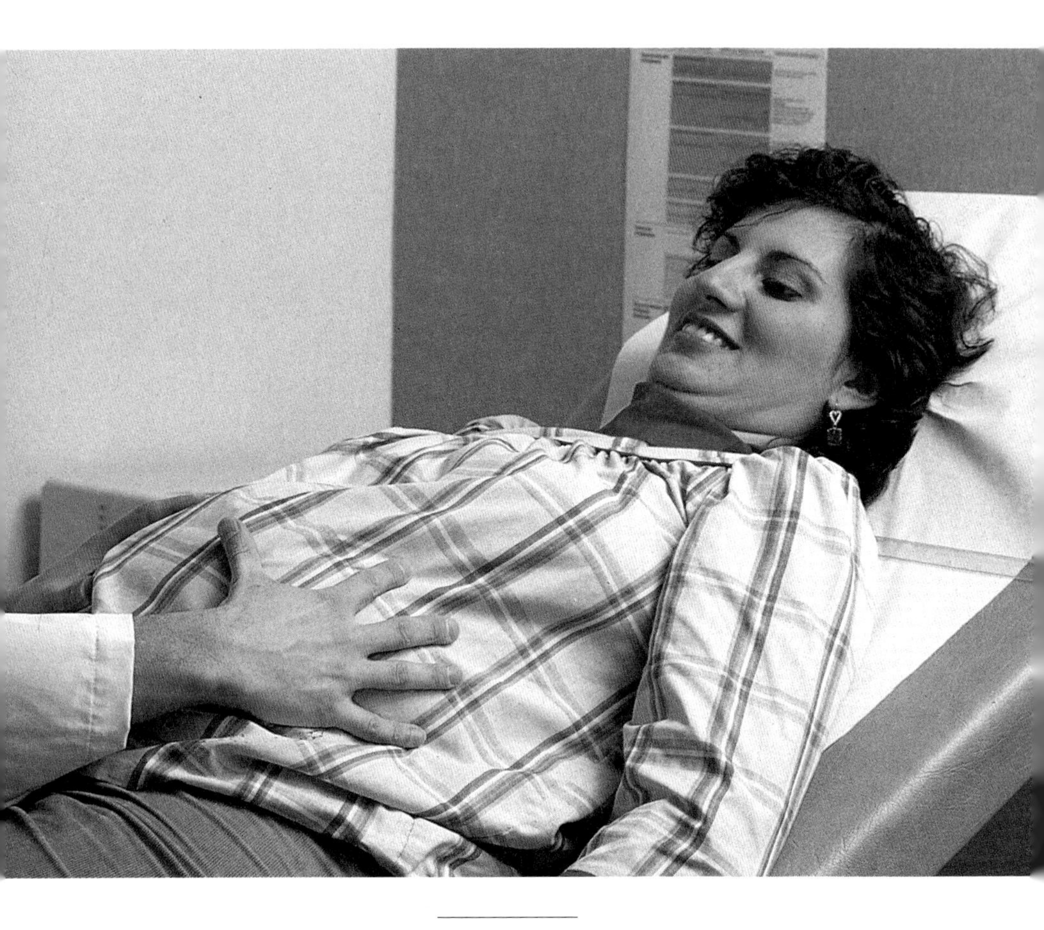

Pregnant women with epilepsy face special concerns and should be carefully monitored by their doctors.

A sudden fall or accident caused by a seizure could hurt the child as well.

Pregnant women with epilepsy should fully discuss the issue with their doctor. Before deciding whether to stay on an antiepileptic drug they must carefully consider all the risks involved. More than 90 percent of the women who continue their medication through their pregnancy have normal, healthy babies.

There are special concerns regarding young children and anticonvulsants as well. It's crucial that children with epilepsy see their doctor regularly since as they grow and gain weight, their medication dosage may no longer be right for them. Children are sometimes given greater amounts of antiepileptic drugs than adults because a higher dose is generally necessary to stop young people's seizures. However, at puberty, this changes as adolescents physically become adults. Therefore if patients don't see their doctor at this point they may become overmedicated. This could result in them feeling exhausted and finding it difficult to pay attention in school.

Having the right medication has made an overwhelming difference in the lives of many people with epilepsy. According to The Epilepsy Institute at least 50 percent of those taking anticonvulsants will experience total seizure control, while another 30 percent achieve partial control. Unfortunately, the remaining 20 percent aren't helped at all by these drugs. A small percentage of those for whom the medication has not been effective have largely stopped their seizures through surgery.

Sadly, there are still approximately 800,000 Americans who are unable to benefit from either surgery or medication. However, epilepsy research continues at the National Institute of Neurological Disorders and Strokes Antiepileptic Drug Development Program, which was established in 1975 as a cooperative effort between the federal government and the drug industry. The program has evaluated more than 16,000 antiepileptic compounds since it was established, and assisted in the development of several commonly prescribed antiepileptic medications. Hopefully one day an effective drug for everyone coping with seizures will be available.

CHAPTER THREE

Surgery

In recent years surgery has become an option for some people with epilepsy who do not respond to drugs. It's estimated that of the 2.5 million people in the United States who have epilepsy, about 100,000 could benefit from this operation. However, to qualify for the procedure, patients must first meet certain conditions. The damaged cells or tissue to be removed must be located in one fairly small area of the brain. The surgeon must also be able to remove this part of the brain without harming the person's mental abilities.

Research to surgically remove damaged brain tissue has been going on for more than 100 years. But until 1990 the National Institutes of Health did not recognize the procedure as an acceptable treatment for people with epilepsy. Today this type of surgery is often thought to be most beneficial to infants and young children. That's because their brains are still growing and the lost brain tissue is readily replaced. Yet surgery to remove damaged tissue has been effective for adults as well.

One neurosurgery success story involved a 12-year-old boy named Andrew Cooke. When Andrew was nine he began having seizures. At first the seizures were fairly mild—the boy would slip into a trancelike state. During these attacks he couldn't talk or move. Afterward he was unable to remember what happened. Andrew didn't know when the seizures were going to occur. There was never any warning beforehand.

As time passed Andrew's seizures grew worse. His mother described the change this way, "He used to just . . . stare at me. . . . Then, as time went on, he started to jerk, you know, he would start moving his right arm, and then after moving his right arm . . . he actually falls down, and he just doesn't respond, he blanks out completely. To me it seems like hours, but it's probably about four minutes."[1]

Andrew soon experienced increasing numbers of seizures as well. Once he began having as many as three attacks a day, his mother became afraid to leave him alone. Although Andrew's school was only three blocks from his home, Mrs. Cooke drove her son back and forth each day.

As she described her feelings about what was happening, "I can't live day to day. I worry about him, he goes to school. I worry by the phone, if the phone is going to ring, that they may call me up and tell me Andrew had his [seizure] on a flight of stairs. That's what I worry about mostly. What happens if he has it on a flight of stairs? He can kill himself."[2]

Andrew couldn't control when or where a seizure would occur. He'd experienced these attacks in a swimming pool, walking down the street, playing with friends, and while alone in his basement. Unfortunately, he also had seizures at the one place he'd wanted to keep his epilepsy a secret—school. Having epilepsy made Andrew feel embarrassed and different from his classmates. "I couldn't do anything about it," he recalled. "Then the kids started making fun of me about it."[3]

Although epileptic seizures can be brought on by a number of environmental factors, Andrew's were triggered by physical activity. This meant that his participation in gym class was limited to keeping score, while the other boys enjoyed various sports. After school Andrew stood on the sidelines and watched his friends play ball in the street.

His father recounted what Andrew's summers were like: "It's very heartbreaking, you know, especially when you see a kid his size, you know, he's a big kid . . . a child his size in a pool and he has to wear a tube, you know, so he won't drown, and somebody has to be ready to jump in and pull him out. . . . As a parent, it's very heartbreaking." Mrs. Cooke added, "And you see envy in his eyes. Kids don't call for him, nobody rings the bell for him. It hurts."[4]

Andrew's parents sought medical help for their son, but at first his future looked bleak. The medication prescribed for the 12-year-old stopped working after a few months. Andrew also had a toxic reaction to the drug. After being on it for a time he could barely walk and he also became delusional.

Following numerous medical consultations Andrew and his parents decided to try the last possible alternative for people in his predicament. They agreed to surgery to remove the damaged brain tissue responsible for the boy's seizures. The procedure is lengthy and requires a good deal of precision and skill on the part of the surgeons performing it. Andrew would need a lot of courage, too. Unlike most operations during which the patient is unconscious, Andrew would be awake and speaking to his doctors during the most of the procedure.

Andrew Cooke's surgery was to be performed at New York University's Hospital for Joint Diseases. On the day of his surgery Andrew was on the operating table by 8:45 A.M. and had been injected with sufficient painkillers to numb the multiple layers of bone and skin protecting the brain. The surgeons operating on Andrew had to be especially careful since testing had shown that the cells to be removed were on the left side of the brain. As that's the side responsible for thinking and communication, it was crucial that these vital functions not be disturbed during the surgery.

To insure that everything went smoothly, Andrew's doctor performed a process known as brain mapping. Using a tiny electric probe, the surgeon identified and labeled the areas of the brain where speech, memory, and understanding occurs. Andrew needed to be alert during the surgery to help the doctor correctly pinpoint these areas.

For example, Andrew was asked to count aloud through part of the operation. When the boy's counting abruptly stopped the surgeon knew he'd located the speech area of his young patient's brain. To assist the doctor in finding the memory center of his brain, Andrew identified pictures on a computer screen.

By four hours into Andrew's eight-hour operation, his brain had been completely mapped. The patient was finally permitted to nap while the doctors proceeded with the surgery. Removing the tissue containing the damaged nerve cells would take about two hours.

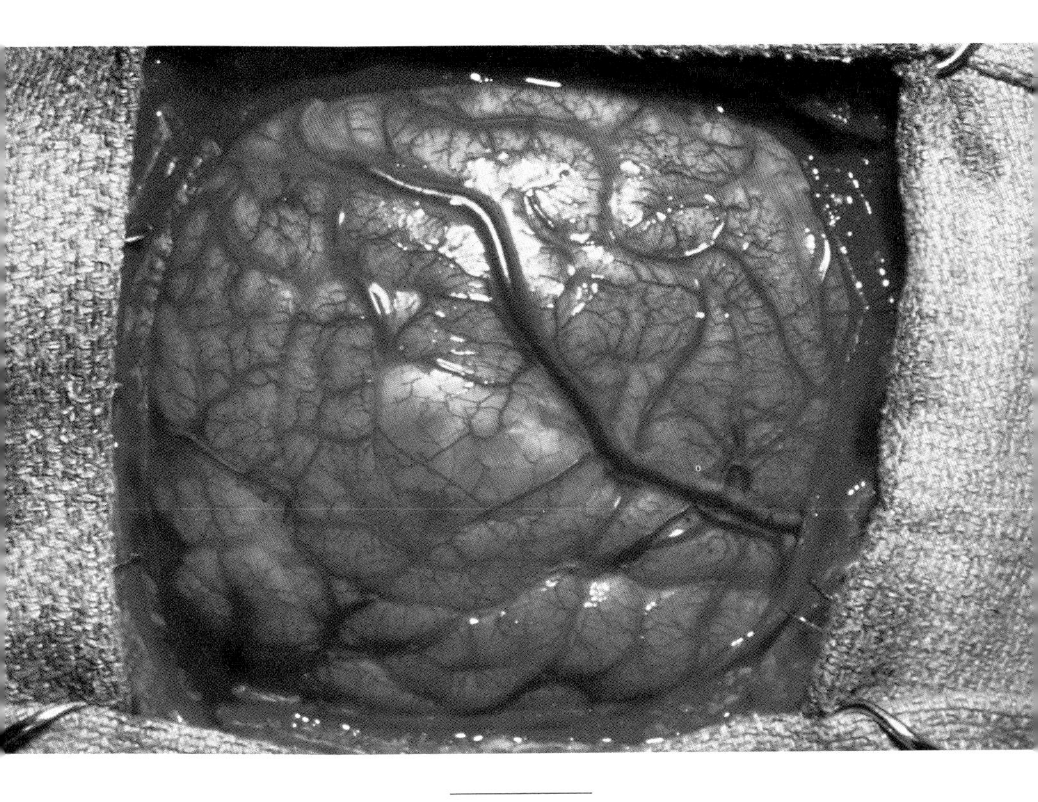

The human brain uncovered in surgery for epilepsy.

Andrew's brain would not be cut—instead the tissue would be sucked out through a tiny device that acts like a vacuum cleaner. This part of the operation was completely painless because there's no feeling in brain tissue. The small hole left in the boy's brain by the removed tissue would fill up with brain fluid.

Andrew Cooke's operation turned out well. His surgeons felt they had removed nearly all the damaged tissue and that Andrew had an 85 percent chance of not having seizures in the future. The boy recovered speedily. Four months later he was walking home from school instead of having his mother drive him. He no longer just watched other boys play ball, now he took part.

"[His doctors] gave Andrew a new life," Mrs. Cooke stated while discussing the surgery's outcome. "He's throwing a ball. . . . He's running. He's playing tackle. I mean he's playing things that he never thought he would do."[5] For the first time in years, Andrew felt free.

Although Andrew and others like him have greatly benefited from the surgery, the idea of removing brain tissue is still troublesome to some individuals. They ask if the patients lose something after the damaged cells are removed and wonder if these individuals will later suffer some unforeseen consequences. However, research has shown this not to be the case. People who volunteered for this surgery while it was still experimental were tracked by researchers for between 5 to 20 years following their operations. Intensive testing revealed that instead of giving something up, in a number of cases the patients' abilities actually improved. This was especially evident in the area of memory.

Another person who feels this surgery dramatically improved her life is Eve Thompson (name changed), a 29-year-old mother of three. When she was 14 Eve suffered a head injury in a car accident, which led to epilepsy. Before long Eve began having seizures and she found that the medication prescribed for her hardly helped.

Nevertheless, Eve tried to lead a normal life. She became a beautician and eventually opened her own

After a successful surgery, a recovered patient can lead a more carefree life.

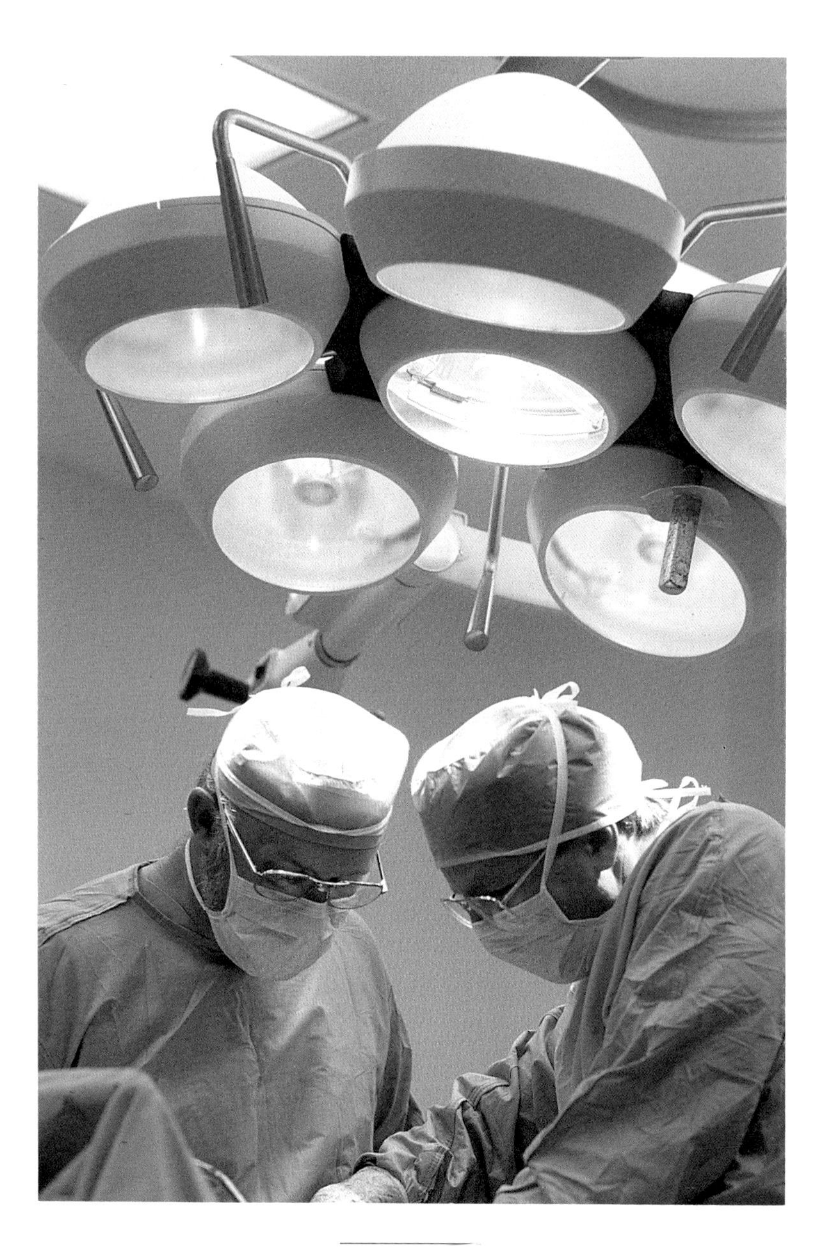

Although surgery is not risk-free, it can be the right choice for some people.

beauty shop. Eve also married the boy she dated in high school and started a family. But during her second pregnancy Eve's seizures became more intense and following the infant's birth, they were more frequent as well. The situation became especially perilous when, while pregnant with her third child, Eve had a seizure driving her two daughters to the babysitter's house. Even though her car collided with four other vehicles, luckily no one was hurt.

It was then that Eve realized she needed to make some changes to insure her family's safety. Although she hated giving up her independence, she now had a neighbor drive her to work and her daughters to nursery school. But soon afterward she found that even this wasn't enough. After her third daughter was born, Eve had a seizure while feeding the newborn baby. Fortunately her other daughters were there to take the infant from their mother's arms as Eve fell to the floor.

Following that incident Eve's husband no longer felt comfortable going off to work and leaving his wife alone. Eve was depressed as well. She was afraid to bathe her children or even take them to the playground, for fear of having a seizure.

She had seen a physician who thought she might be helped by surgery, but at first Eve hesitated. She knew that the operation wasn't risk-free. If something went wrong, she might be left partially paralyzed or speech impaired. Eve especially feared the possibility of losing her memory, since she cherished all the wonderful experiences she had shared with her husband and daughters.

Yet after discussing her options with her family, Eve decided to have the surgery. She'd been willing to tolerate occasional mild seizures, but now Eve felt that epilepsy was robbing her of her life. Fortunately, the operation was a success—Eve completely recovered and has not had a single seizure since. Today she feels that she can once again be a mother to her children, a wife to her husband, and a fulfilled individual.

CHAPTER FOUR

The Facts About Epilepsy

People with epilepsy not only have to cope with seizures and the sometimes unpleasant side effects of medication. They must deal with the social stigma attached to the disorder. Unfortunately, negative myths about epilepsy still exist. Dr. Orrin Devinsky, director of the Epilepsy Center at New York University Hospital for Joint Diseases noted, "People think of it [epilepsy] as associated with insanity, associated with very low intelligence, or violence. Again, it's just a misconception that doesn't go away."[1]

At times people feel needlessly anxious about being around someone who has epilepsy. Seeing a seizure can sometimes be unsettling to people who don't really understand what's happening. As Dr. Jeanne Ann King, a neurologist at the University of Oklahoma Health Sciences Center put it, "Control is a very important thing to people. To see someone fall down out of control or go into a trancelike state is frightening to observers."[2]

Knowledge can go a long way in dispelling myths about epilepsy. See how many of the following true or false statements you can answer correctly.

Epilepsy is a rare and unusual disorder.

False. Epilepsy affects people of all races in nations throughout the world. Although it can occur at any time in a person's life, often young people are affected. About 30 percent of all people with epilepsy have their first seizure before they are five years old. Of all Americans who have epilepsy, more than a third of them are children. The disorder affects boys and girls equally.

Epilepsy is highly contagious. If you get too close to someone having a seizure, you can come down with the disorder as well.

False. Epilepsy is not infectious. You can't "catch" epilepsy from a person who has it. This is true regardless of whether you swim in the same pool, sit next to that person at school, or eat lunch together.

Epilepsy is inherited. If someone with the disorder has a child, it's likely that the child will have epilepsy as well.

False. Although the child of someone with this disorder has a slightly higher chance of having epilepsy, it's far more likely that he or she will not.

However, other elements are involved in its onset. While in 50 percent of the cases epilepsy's cause remains unknown, frequently the factors listed below play a role:

- Head injury. A severe head injury or trauma brought on as the result of an automobile or motorcycle collision, a fall, or sports accident is frequently cited as a cause of epilepsy. Blows or gunshot wounds to the head can have the same effect.
- Lead poisoning, serious vitamin deficiencies, and fluctuations in blood sugar levels (such as

Severe head injuries resulting from sports accidents are a common cause of epilepsy.

those experienced by people with diabetes) can lead to epilepsy in some cases.

- Illness. At times epilepsy has surfaced after a major illness such as meningitis, viral encephalitis (inflammation of the brain), measles, mumps, diphtheria, or a severe infection. Some pregnant women who experience a serious illness or injury may give birth to a child who develops epilepsy early in infancy.

There is nothing anyone can do to prevent epilepsy.

False. According to The Epilepsy Institute "anything that can injure the brain can [also] cause epilepsy." Therefore following these safety precautions and good health practices recommended by the institute can go a long way in lessening the new cases of epilepsy that occur each year.

- All vehicles, including motorcycles and bicycles, should be driven safely. Use seat belts, observe speed limits, and wear helmets where appropriate.
- Minimize (lessen) the risks involved in recreational activities. Wear protective headgear for bicycling, skateboarding, football, and baseball. Play it safe when diving or climbing, et cetera.
- Use drugs only as prescribed.
- Immunize children against infectious diseases.

A person who has epilepsy can feel a seizure coming on and prevent it if he or she concentrates hard enough.

False. Some people who have seizures experience an aura (an unusual sensation) before the attack begins. The aura may take the form of a strange taste or smell, thereby allowing the person to try to move away from objects

Using a seat belt helps prevent head injuries that can lead to epilepsy. Very small children should always ride in car seats.

that could pose a danger as he or she falls. However, the individual is unable to stop the seizure.

People with epilepsy don't always survive a severe seizure.

False. Although someone may look quite ill during a seizure, these attacks are rarely fatal. Death resulting from seizures usually only occurs if the person experiences a series of ongoing seizures lasting for several hours. However, even these fatalities can frequently be prevented if the individual receives emergency medical treatment.

There are certain "triggers" that can bring on seizures in people who have epilepsy.

True. While there is no one thing that will cause every person with epilepsy to have a seizure, some patients react to certain seizure "triggers." Some of the more commonly identified triggers include flickering lights such as strobes or even sunlight flickering through tree leaves, hunger, exhaustion, and forgetting to take prescribed antiepileptic drugs.

Perhaps just as important as knowing the facts about epilepsy is knowing what to do as well as what not to do if someone has a convulsive or tonic-clonic seizure. In such instances following these guidelines can be extremely helpful:

- Remain calm.
- If the person senses the seizure coming on early enough you may be able to help the person lower him- or herself to the floor or ground.
- Do not try to hold down or restrain someone having a seizure. Once a seizure has begun there's no way to stop it or lessen its force.
- Push away any sharp or dangerous objects near the person that could pierce, poke, or fall on the individual. Although you can move

CHAPTER FIVE

Overcoming Obstacles

It started on an ordinary evening as 13-year-old Jennifer sat down to dinner with her parents and younger brother. The girl didn't understand precisely what was happening but she mentioned to her parents that somehow her tongue felt as though she'd bitten it. At the time no one knew what was the matter, but before long the situation became clear. Several minutes later Jennifer had her first seizure.

As her father described it, "Jennifer's arms flew up and her body jerked and she crashed to the floor, shaken into unconsciousness in the hands of an invisible raging giant. I felt helpless, unable to do more than cradle my daughter's head on my knees."[1]

Jennifer had epilepsy and as time passed the young teen and her family learned a great deal about the "giant" that had unexpectedly gripped the girl that day. While trying to adjust to the antiepileptic drugs prescribed for her, Jennifer experienced some difficulties. Plagued by the medication's side effects, her grades dropped, and she fell down a flight of steps at school. At that point the school administration considered putting Jennifer in a class for students with learning disabilities even though epilepsy does not make a person learning disabled. Fortunately, they decided against it.

"On the whole, my teachers made sincere attempts at being understanding," Jennifer recalled. "Some seemed afraid of epilepsy. They'd tell me not to worry about doing my homework or taking tests on time. Others were overly demanding and wouldn't accept reasons for late or poor work. After I fell down the stairs, I wasn't allowed to walk to or from class by myself, and I had to leave classes early to avoid the rush of students. It was frustrating."[2]

Jennifer wasn't the only one in her family who had to learn to cope with the everyday frustrations that sometimes accompany epilepsy. Her younger brother was frightened by her seizures and didn't want to talk about them. Her parents, on the other hand, tended to be overprotective. Nevertheless, after a while, Jennifer began to resume the lifestyle she'd had before her first seizure. She managed to earn honor grades at prep school and be accepted at a fine college in Baltimore, Maryland.

Jennifer left for college with her parents' warning not to do anything that could trigger a seizure. But she was determined to live her life as a normal person and make the most of her time at school. As she said, "I never thought the best solution was to have a limited life. I'd rather do things and take risks than do nothing at all. Going to college far from home wasn't something I felt afraid of. I felt very capable of taking care of myself."[3]

Jennifer, like many other young people with epilepsy, proved to be just that: capable. For almost two years she remained seizure-free. Then when she had a seizure while showering at her dormitory, she had a friend call her family to assure them that she was fine. Jennifer's parents realized that their daughter was successfully coping with her disorder while away at school. She had taken an important step toward independence.

Today as an adult Jennifer has come to grips with having epilepsy. She's achieved many of the goals she set for herself—including going mountain climbing with a group of skilled mountaineers. Jennifer refused to let epilepsy limit her life. As she explained, "Although I've felt frustrated and occasionally angry, I've never felt embarrassed. I have epilepsy, but epilepsy doesn't have me."[4]

While countless individuals like Jennifer have overcome their disorder, frequently society still sets obstacles in their paths. Although people with epilepsy do not differ in intelligence or emotional well-being from anyone else, they are often still treated as though they do. Despite medical and technological advances, unfortunately societal attitudes lag behind. Until the mid-1960s some states did not even allow people with epilepsy to marry.

At times individuals who have epilepsy have faced serious job discrimination. That's what happened to Mr. S. who'd successfully worked as a toll booth clerk in the New York City subway system for a number of years. When Mr. S. was hired he did not mention that he had epilepsy as he was not legally obligated to do so. He'd been seizure-free on antiepileptic drugs for some time, and after his first year with the subway system had received an excellent job performance rating.

However, when his toll booth was robbed, Mr. S. was required to take a drug test as a matter of procedure. Unfortunately, his antiepileptic medication showed up on the test and he was suspected of taking illegal drugs. Following the test results, Mr. S. was promptly placed on involuntary medical leave for two months.

In trying to explain what had occurred, Mr. S. revealed to his employer, the Metropolitan Transit Authority, that he had epilepsy. His supervisors had him see a company neurologist who took him off his medication since Mr. S. hadn't had a seizure in years. Mr. S. went along with the physician's decision, but shortly afterward, he had his first seizure in eight years.

Following Mr. S.'s seizure another Transit Authority doctor ruled that he wasn't fit for work in a single-person toll booth. This placed his job at risk since there were only a few booths where more than one clerk worked. According to Transit Authority policy, Mr. S. would be kept on leave without pay until there was an opening in a two-person booth. If that didn't occur within a year, he'd be laid off.

In response, Mr. S. contacted The Epilepsy Institute, which led to his working with the New York Legal Aid Society Civil Appeals and Law Reform Unit. The attorneys attained a favorable settlement for Mr. S. based on the Rehabilitation Act of 1973 and the New York State Human Rights Law. They successfully showed that Mr. S.'s work in a single-person toll booth had always been more than acceptable.[5]

It's sad that cases like Mr. S.'s still occur, but they do. Throughout history many people with epilepsy have made brilliant and highly valued contributions in both the arts and sciences. Among these are the talented French writer Gustave Flaubert (1821-1880), whose vivid and lifelike novels made him internationally famous and

Self-portrait of Vincent van Gogh

Fyodor Dostoyevsky (1821-1881), a novelist and considered one of the greatest Russian writers. George Frideric Handel (1685-1759) the acclaimed German composer who wrote more than 40 operas and the famous musical composition the *Messiah*, had epilepsy as well. So did the colorful English poet Lord George Byron (1788-1824), and the outstanding Dutch painter Vincent van Gogh (1853-1890), who is among the most famous painters in modern art. People with epilepsy are still barred from the United States Armed Forces, yet some of the greatest commanders-in-chief in history, such as Alexander the Great, Julius Caesar, and Napoleon Bonaparte, had this disorder.[6]

It's important to break down age-old myths that destroy dreams and limit lives. People with epilepsy can be wonderful employees, friends, spouses, and parents. As The Epilepsy Institute reminds us, "They are just people. Epilepsy is something they have, not something they are. The real challenge to them—and to society—is to recognize that simple fact."[7]

END NOTES

CHAPTER 1

1. Sheryl DeVore, "The Facts of Life with Epilepsy," *Current Health 2*, January 1989, 10.

2. Ibid.

3. National Institute of Neurological Disorders and Strokes, *Epilepsy: Hope Through Research* (Bethesda, Md.: National Institutes of Health 1981), 2.

CHAPTER 2

1. National Institute of Neurological Disorders and Strokes/National Institutes of Health. Press Release. August 2, 1993.

CHAPTER 3

1. *20/20*, "A New Life for Andrew, Part I," March 1, 1991.

2. Ibid.

3. Ibid.

4. Ibid.

5. Ibid.

CHAPTER 4

1. *20/20*, "A New Life for Andrew, Part I," March 1, 1991.

2. "Cutting Through the Myths," *USA Today,* October 7, 1992.

Chapter 5

1. John Lovell and Jennifer Lovell, "I Am Not Defined By My Disorder," *Parade,* August 15, 1993, 6.

2. Ibid.

3. Ibid.

4. Ibid.

5. The Epilepsy Institute, *Understanding Epilepsy: An Information Resource for People with Epilepsy, Their Families and the Community,* Vol. 1, No. 1, New York: The Epilepsy Institute, 1993, 5.

6. Ibid.

7. The Epilepsy Institute, *Epilepsy: Breaking Down the Walls of Misunderstanding,* New York: The Epilepsy Institute, unpaged.

GLOSSARY

absence seizure—a kind of epileptic seizure in which the person is momentarily dazed. This kind of seizure may even go unnoticed.

antiepileptic medication (also known as anticonvulsants)—drugs prescribed to prevent seizures

aura—an unusual sensation, such as a peculiar odor or a flash of light, that some people with epilepsy experience just before a seizure

biofeedback—a technique in which a person learns to control his or her biological processes, such as brain waves, blood pressure, and skin temperature, and to lower these processes to a more relaxed level

brain mapping—the technique of identifying and labeling the areas of the brain. During brain mapping, the patient's brain is exposed and the surgeon pinpoints areas of the brain with a tiny electric probe. The patient must be alert so the surgeon may correctly locate each area of the brain.

CAT scan (computerized axial tomography)—a computerized three-dimensional X-ray image of the brain used to help diagnose various medical conditions

disoriented—to be confused as to location or direction

EEG (electroencephalogram)—a test used to detect abnormal brain cell activity by recording the electrical charges that pass between brain cells

epilepsy—the medical term used to describe a number of disorders that are largely characterized by seizures

hallucination—seeing or hearing something that isn't there

ketogenic diet—a diet rich in fat and calories that alters the body's chemistry to prevent seizures. This diet is sometimes prescribed for young people with epilepsy for whom medication has not been successful, but is not a common form of treatment.

MRI (magnetic resonance imaging)—a diagnostic technique that uses magnetic fields to provide a highly detailed picture of the brain

neurologist—a doctor specializing in diseases and disorders of the brain and nervous system

neurons—nerve cells

PET (positron-emission tomography) scan—a method used to obtain color-coded, three-dimensional pictures of a solid object, such as a brain

sedative—a medication that calms and soothes

stigma—a mark of disgrace or shame

tonic-clonic seizure—a violent epileptic seizure in which the person may thrash about wildly

FURTHER READING

NONFICTION

Bergman, Thomas. *Moments that Disappear.* Milwaukee: Gareth Stevens Childrens Books 1992.

Facklam, Margery, and Howard Facklam. *The Brain: Magnificent Mind Machine.* New York: Harcourt Brace and Jovanovich, 1982.

Krementz, Jill. *How It Feels to Live with a Physical Disability.* New York: Simon and Schuster, 1992.

McGowan, Tom. *Epilepsy.* New York, Franklin Watts, 1989.

Parker, Steve. *The Brain and the Nervous System.* New York: Franklin Watts, 1990.

Sands, Harry, and Frances C. Minters. *The Epilepsy Fact Book: A Complete Guide to the Most Misunderstood Physical Disorder.* New York: Scribner's, 1979.

Silverstein, Alvin, and Virginia B. Silverstein. *Epilepsy.* New York: HarperCollins, 1990.

FICTION

Hall, Lynn. *Halsey's Pride.* New York: Scribner's, 1990.

Howard, Ellen. *Edith Herself.* New York, Atheneum, 1987.

Jones, Rebecca C. *Madeline and the Great Escape Artist.* New York: Dutton, 1983.

Sherburne, Zoa. *Why Have the Birds Stopped Singing?* New York: Morrow, 1974.

ORGANIZATONS
CONCERNED WITH EPILEPSY

American Epilepsy Society
638 Prospect Avenue
Hartford, CT 06105-4298

Epilepsy Concern Group
1283 Wynnewood Drive
West Palm Beach, FL 33417

Epilepsy Foundation of America
4351 Garden City Drive
Landover, MD 20785

The Epilepsy Institute
257 Park Avenue
New York, NY 10010

International League Against Epilepsy
National Institutes of Health
Bldg. 31, Room 8A52
Bethesda, MD 20824

INDEX